I0813899

ST. LOUIS CARDINALS

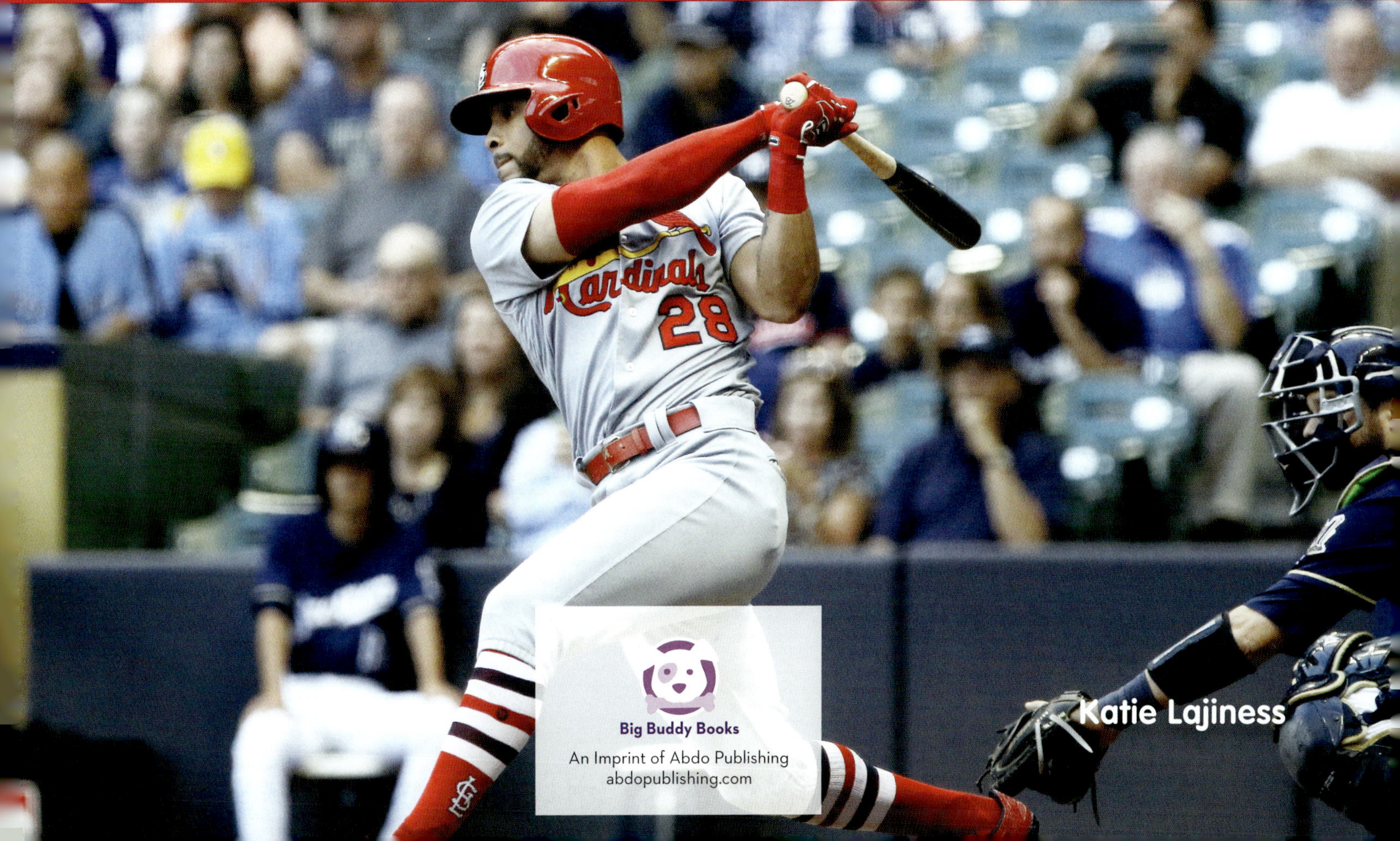

Katie Lajiness

Big Buddy Books
An Imprint of Abdo Publishing
abdopublishing.com

abdopublishing.com

Published by Abdo Publishing, a division of ABDO, PO Box 398166, Minneapolis, Minnesota 55439.

Printed in the United States of America, North Mankato, Minnesota.
052018
092018

Cover Photo: Dylan Buell/Getty Images.
Interior Photos: 33ft/Depositphotos (p. 7); AP Images (pp. 19, 21, 22, 28); Doug Pensinger/Getty Images (p. 17); Elsa/Getty Images (p. 5); Ezra Shaw/Getty Images (p. 15); Jeff Curry/Getty Images (p. 9); Joe Sargent/Getty Images (p. 29); JP/AP Images (p. 11); Maddie Meyer/Getty Images (p. 27); Matthew Stockman/Getty Images (pp. 24, 25); Susan Walsh/AP Images (p. 23); Tom Hauck/Getty Images (p. 23); Vincent Laforet/Getty Images (p. 13).

Coordinating Series Editor: Tamara L. Britton
Graphic Design: Jenny Christensen

Library of Congress Control Number: 2017962680

Publisher's Cataloging-in-Publication Data

Names: Lajiness, Katie, author.
Title: St. Louis Cardinals / by Katie Lajiness.
Description: Minneapolis, Minnesota : Abdo Publishing, 2019. | Series: MLB's greatest teams | Includes online resources and index.
Identifiers: ISBN 9781532115202 (lib.bdg.) | ISBN 9781532155925 (ebook)
Subjects: LCSH: Major League Baseball (Organization)--Juvenile literature. | Baseball teams--United States--History--Juvenile literature. | St. Louis Cardinals (Baseball team)--Juvenile literature. | Sports teams--Juvenile literature.
Classification: DDC 796.35764--dc23

Contents

Major League Baseball 4
A Winning Team. 6
Busch Stadium. 8
Then and Now. 10
Highlights 14
Famous Managers 18
Star Players 22
Final Call 26
Through the Years. 28
Glossary 30
Online Resources 31
Index 32

Major League Baseball

League Play

There are two leagues in MLB. They are the American League (AL) and the National League (NL). Each league has 15 teams and is split into three divisions. They are east, central, and west.

The St. Louis Cardinals is one of 30 Major League Baseball (MLB) teams. The team plays in the National League Central **Division**.

Throughout the season, all MLB teams play 162 games. The season begins in April and can continue until November.

The Cardinals mascot Fredbird hatched in April 1979.

A Winning Team

The Cardinals team is from St. Louis, Missouri. The team's colors are white, Cardinal red, and navy blue.

The team has had good seasons and bad. But time and again, the Cardinals players have proven themselves. Let's see what makes the Cardinals one of MLB's greatest teams!

Fast Facts

HOME FIELD: Busch Stadium

TEAM COLORS: White, Cardinal red, and navy blue

TEAM SONG: "For My Cards" by Code Red

PENNANTS: 23

WORLD SERIES TITLES: 1926, 1931, 1934, 1942, 1944, 1946, 1964, 1967, 1982, 2006, 2011

CANADA
UNITED STATES OF AMERICA
MEXICO
Nebraska
Iowa
Illinois
Kansas
St. Louis
Missouri
Kentucky
Oklahoma
Arkansas
Tennessee
N
W
E
S

Busch Stadium

The team began playing at Sportsman's Park in 1920. Over the next 20 years, team owners rebuilt the park to make it larger. The Cardinals hosted the 1944 World Series at the updated park.

In 1953, Sportsman's Park was renamed Busch Stadium. The first Busch Stadium closed in 1966 and was replaced by the Busch Memorial Stadium. The team played there from 1966 to 2005.

Then in 2006, the Cardinals began playing at the third Busch Stadium. The newest stadium holds nearly 44,000 fans.

The Cardinals' biggest rival is the Chicago Cubs.

Then and Now

The St. Louis Brown Stockings began in 1882 as part of the American Association. Ten years later, the team joined the NL. That is the league in which it still plays.

The Cardinals have had a few different names throughout the years. In 1883, the Brown Stockings became the St. Louis Browns. Later, a news reporter called the team the Cardinals in a 1900 news article. The name stuck and it has been the team's name ever since.

First baseman Johnny Mize joined the team in 1936. He was called "The Big Cat" because of the graceful way he moved around the field.

During the 1940s, the team won 960 games. It was one of the most successful decades in team history. In 1953, Gussie Busch became team president. He led the Cardinals to more wins, including two World Series in 1964 and 1967.

By the 1970s, the team struggled on the field. But the Cardinals found their way back with a World Series win in 1982. And, the team scored a **pennant** in 1987.

The 1990s was another tough decade for the Cardinals. But in 2004, the team won its first pennant in 17 years. And in 2006, it won its first World Series since 1982.

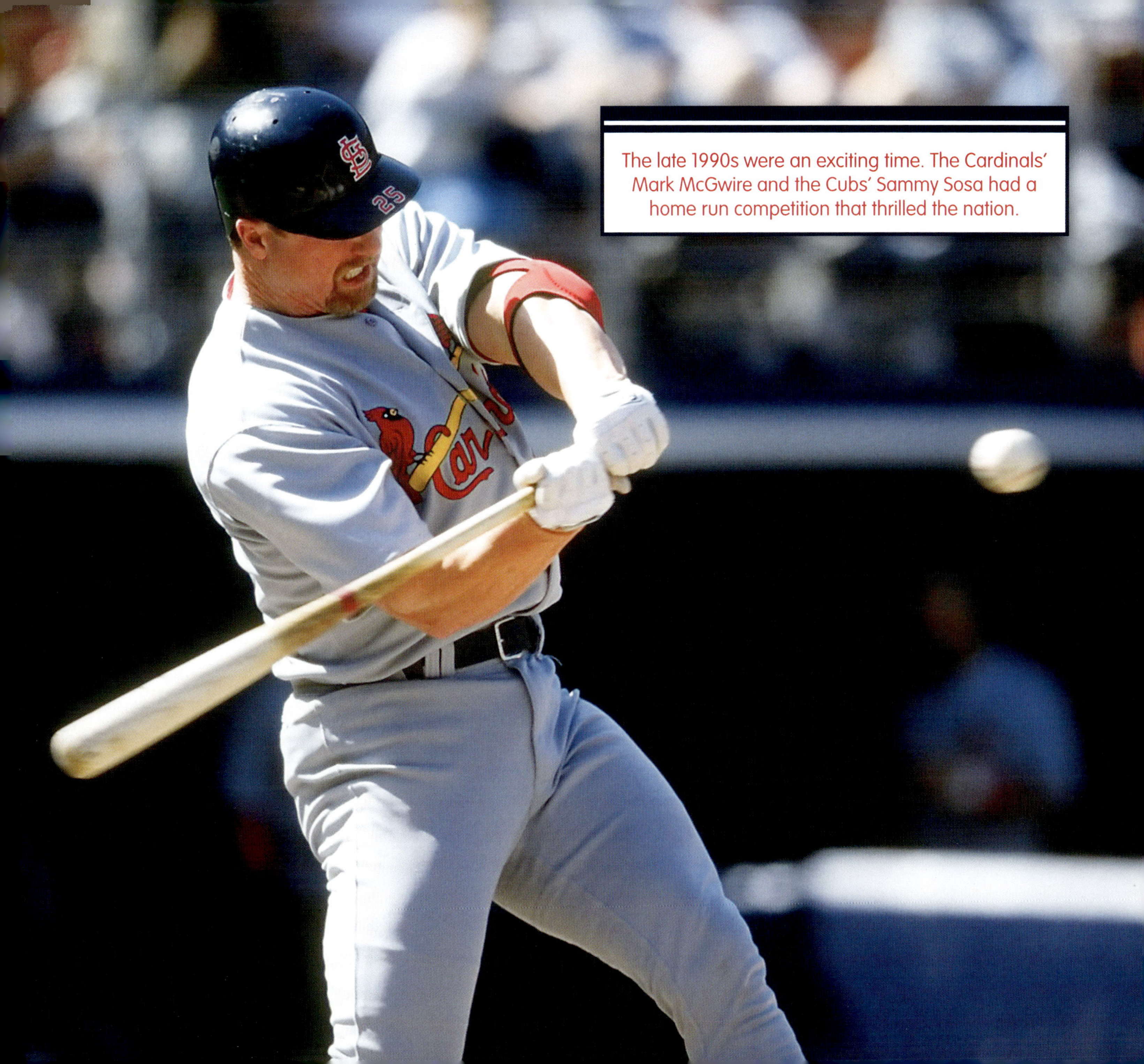

The late 1990s were an exciting time. The Cardinals' Mark McGwire and the Cubs' Sammy Sosa had a home run competition that thrilled the nation.

Highlights

Throughout history, the Cardinals have had many wins. As the St. Louis Browns, the team won four **pennants**. Since becoming the Cardinals, it has won 19 pennants. And, the team has finished in first place 25 times.

There are 50 former Cardinals players and managers in the National Baseball Hall of Fame. The Hall of Fame Museum is located in Cooperstown, New York.

Win or Go Home

The top team from each AL and NL division goes to the playoffs. Each league also sends one wild-card team. One team from the AL and one from the NL will win the pennant. The two pennant winners then go to the World Series!

The Cardinals have played in more than 60 **playoff** games since 2009. That is more than any MLB team over the past five seasons.

In total, the team has won 11 World Series titles. Its most recent World Series win was in 2011. The team won in Game Seven over the Texas Rangers.

The Cardinals team has won more World Series titles than any other NL team.

Famous Managers

Frankie Frisch played second base with St. Louis from 1927 to 1933. Then, he acted as both player and manager until 1938. Frisch played in 50 World Series games throughout his **career**.

As both player and manager, Frisch won two World Series with the Cardinals. He earned the Cardinals' **Most Valuable Player (MVP)** Award in 1931. And in 1935, he took part in his third-straight All-Star Game.

Frisch (*right*) joined the National Baseball Hall of Fame in 1947.

Coach Red Schoendienst began managing the Cardinals in 1965. He led the team to two straight **pennant** wins. And one of those pennants led to the 1967 World Series title.

After 14 seasons with the Cardinals, Schoendienst had brought the team to 1,041 wins. He earned a spot in the National Baseball Hall of Fame in 1989.

Schoendienst (*right*) found success as both a player and a manager. He played second base for the Cardinals for 14 years.

Star Players

Stan Musial LEFT FIELDER, #6

Stan Musial began his **career** as a left-handed pitcher in 1938. He led the team to three World Series titles in five years. In 1948, he won his third **MVP** Award. And, he was only one home run away from a **Triple Crown**. Musial was **inducted** into the National Baseball Hall of Fame in 1969.

Bob Gibson PITCHER, #45

Bob Gibson made his major league appearance in 1959. In the 1964 World Series, he helped win Game Five against the New York Yankees. He pitched again in Game Seven on only two days rest. This led to a Cardinals World Series victory! For that, he earned the World Series MVP Award.

Ozzie Smith SHORTSTOP, #1

Ozzie Smith won 13 **Gold Glove Awards** during his time with the Cardinals. He also led the team to three NL **pennants** and one World Series title. As a shortstop, Smith set MLB records for getting 8,375 assists. In 2002, Smith was **inducted** into the National Baseball Hall of Fame.

1982 – 1996

Mark McGwire FIRST BASEMAN, #25

1997 – 2001

The Cardinals traded for Mark McGwire in 1997. A star player, he hit 220 home runs during his five seasons with the team. He and Cubs player Sammy Sosa had a **competition** for who could hit more home runs. McGwire also showed his skills by taking part in 12 All-Star Games.

2004 –

Yadier Molina CATCHER, #4

In 2000, the St. Louis Cardinals **drafted** Yadier Molina. He made his first MLB appearance in 2004. Molina played on World Series winning teams in 2006 and 2011. He also took part in All-Star Games from 2009 to 2015, and again in 2017. For eight years in a row, Molina has won the NL **Gold Glove Award**.

Adam Wainwright PITCHER, #50

Adam Wainwright began playing with the Cardinals in 2005. He has been a star pitcher ever since. Wainwright earned the 2015 Hutch Award, one of the top awards given to a MLB player. Throughout his **career**, he has struck out more than 1,500 batters. And he can throw a fastball 92 miles (148 km) per hour!

2005 –

Tommy Pham LEFT FIELDER, #28

The Cardinals chose Tommy Pham during the 2006 **draft**. But he made his first MLB appearance in 2014. Despite having a serious eye condition, Pham has hit 33 home runs throughout his MLB **career**. In his fourth season, he had 73 **runs batted in (RBIs)**.

2014 –

Paul DeJong SHORTSTOP, #11

2017 –

In July 2017, Paul DeJong set a **rookie** record by hitting eight home runs. For his accomplishment, he earned NL Rookie of the Month. Later, DeJong hit 14 home runs in his first 53 MLB games. After only one year, he is on his way to becoming one of the most successful players in Cardinals history.

Final Call

All-Stars

The best players from both leagues come together each year for the All-Star Game. This game does not count toward the regular season records. It is simply to celebrate the best players in MLB.

The St. Louis Cardinals have a long, rich history. The team has played in 19 World Series, and it has won 11 titles.

Even during losing seasons, true fans have stuck by the team. Many believe the Cardinals will remain one of the greatest teams in MLB.

In 2017, Tommy Pham hit 23 home runs and stole 25 bases. For this, he was a finalist for the Hank Aaron Award.

Through the Years

1900

The Perfectos officially changed their name to the Cardinals.

1926

In their first World Series, the Cardinals beat the Yankees in Game Seven. The team led the NL with 90 home runs.

1934

The Cardinals did not **broadcast** any of the season's games on the radio. So, attendance levels dropped quite a bit.

1948

Stan Musial won his third NL **MVP** Award.

1968

The Cardinals won their second **pennant** in a row.

1989

The team set a record with more than 3 million fans attending games during the season.

1999

Mark McGwire led the league with 65 home runs.

2005

From 2005 to 2010, Albert Pujols was the top Cardinals player. For his all-star abilities, he earned the Major League Player of the Year Award.

2017

Catcher Yadier Molina announced that he will **retire** in 2021. That means he will spend his entire **career** with the Cardinals.

Glossary

broadcast to send out by radio or television from a transmitting station.

career a period of time spent in a certain job.

competition (kahm-puh-TIH-shuhn) a contest between two or more persons or groups.

division a number of teams grouped together in a sport for competitive purposes.

draft a system for professional sports teams to choose new players.

Gold Glove Award annually given to the MLB players with the best fielding experience.

induct to officially introduce someone as a member.

Most Valuable Player (MVP) the player who contributes the most to his or her team's success.

pennant the prize that is awarded to the champions of the two MLB leagues each year.

playoffs a game or series of games to determine a championship or to break a tie.

rookie a player who is new to the major leagues until he meets certain criteria.

retire to give up one's job.

run batted in (RBI) a run that is scored as a result of a batter's hit, walk, or stolen base.

Triple Crown the achievement of a baseball player who at the end of a season leads the league in batting average, home runs, and runs batted in.

Online Resources

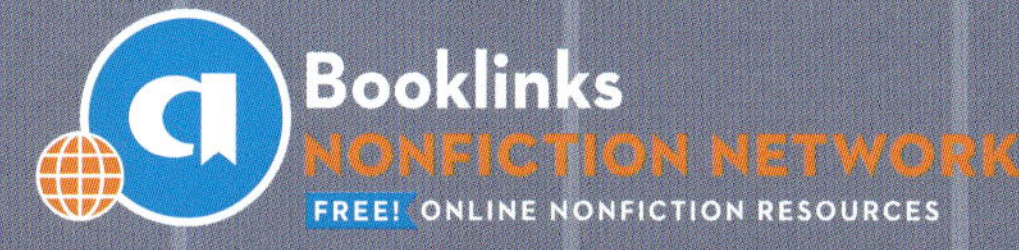

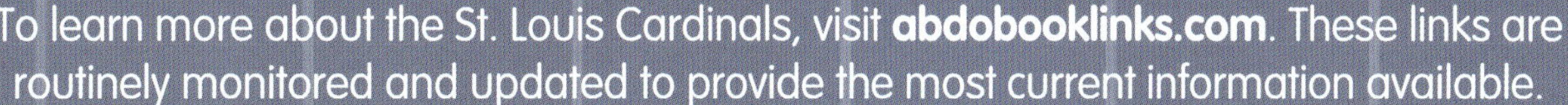
To learn more about the St. Louis Cardinals, visit **abdobooklinks.com**. These links are routinely monitored and updated to provide the most current information available.

Index

All-Star Game **18, 23, 24, 26**
awards **18, 22, 23, 24, 25, 27, 28, 29**
ballparks **6, 8**
Bonds, Barry **13, 23**
Busch, Gussie **12**
Code Red **6**
DeJong, Paul **25**
divisions **4, 14, 16, 26**
"For My Cards" (song) **6**
Frisch, Frankie **18, 19**
Gibson, Bob **22**
Hall of Fame Museum, The **15**
leagues **4, 10, 16, 17, 28**
mascots **5**
McGwire, Mark **13, 23, 24, 25, 26, 29**
Missouri **6**
Mize, Johnny **10**
Molina, Yadier **24, 29**
Musial, Stan **22, 28**
National Baseball Hall of Fame **15, 19, 20, 22, 23**
New York **15**
pennants **6, 12, 14, 20, 23, 28**
Pham, Tommy **25, 27**
playoffs **16**
Pujols, Albert **29**
Schoendienst, Red **20, 21**
Smith, Ozzie **23**
teams **9, 10, 13, 14, 16, 17, 22, 23, 28**
Wainwright, Adam **24**
World Series **6, 8, 12, 16, 17, 18, 20, 22, 23, 24, 26, 27**